"For the forests that v
roam in shadow,and t
in the extrac

Bigfoot Vs Werewolves
Book one of the Bigfoot Vs Series
Written, designed and illustrated by:
B. Humphrey

The Keeper's Tale

The campfire crackled softly, its flames licking the cool mountain air with hues of gold and orange. Shadows danced across the ancient trees, their gnarled branches framing the night like the walls of an eternal cathedral. The woods were alive with the hum of crickets, the faint rustle of leaves, and the distant whisper of a stream winding its way through the heart of the forest.

And there, at the edge of the firelight, sat Koda.

His form was immense, a silhouette that seemed carved from the earth itself. Fur as dark as the forest at midnight, eyes that glimmered like embers reflecting countless years, and a stillness that could silence the wind. Yet, there was a kindness to him, a weightless wisdom that hung in the air like the scent of pine after a rainstorm.

He leaned forward, the firelight catching the edges of his weathered face, casting deep shadows in the lines that spoke of ages lived and battles endured. When he spoke, his voice was a rumble, deep and resonant, like the earth shifting beneath your feet. It wasn't loud, but it carried.

"I remember when the troubles first started," he began, his words slow, deliberate. "The forest whispered it to me in the trembling of leaves, in the rush of a stream that flowed too fast, too nervous—water knows when something is wrong. You can feel it if

you let it run over your hand. Most folks don't listen. But I have to. That's why I'm here."

Koda paused, his massive hand reaching for a branch near the fire, not to stoke it, but to draw its warmth into the stillness of his frame.

"Been here longer than I can say," he continued. "Longer than the stars have known their constellations. My name? Well, my real name... it's older than your words, longer than your breath could carry, and not something your ears could hold." He tilted his head slightly, as if testing the night for the sound of something distant. *"But names are only as heavy as the meaning we give them. You can call me Koda. That'll do just fine."*

The fire crackled in agreement, sparks rising to the dark canopy above.

"There was a man once," Koda said, leaning back into the shadows, his voice softening as though to honor the memory. *"A wise soul from the Miami People. Their Sagamore. Mihšihkinaahkwa. You'd know him as Little Turtle. He was a leader, a protector of his own kind, just as I am of mine."*

Koda's gaze flicked upward, catching the faint glow of the moonlight filtering through the leaves. "He saw me once, not with fear or wonder, but with understanding. We spoke, though words were barely needed. He called me Koda. It means friend or companion in his tongue. And I graciously accepted. It was the kind of name you carry with you, not because it was given, but because it fit."

"I've walked this land since the rivers carved their paths," Koda continued, *"since the sky danced with colors even the boldest sunsets have forgotten. They call me Bigfoot."* His lips curled into something resembling a smile. *"Some with fear, some with*

wonder, and some with a child's curiosity. Truth is, I am all they see and none of it. I'm what they need me to be. Protector, spirit, shadow—whatever fits the story they're telling themselves when they catch a glimpse of me through the trees."

He waved a massive hand toward the woods beyond the firelight. *"I don't mind the stories. They don't bother me. What does bother me is when the balance shifts, when the old things that sleep too lightly wake with a hunger that burns. That's when I step in, not to harm, but to remind. Everything has its place, even the monsters. But sometimes, they need a firmer hand to show them where they belong."*

"The woods know me," Koda said, his voice carrying a weight that silenced the crickets for a moment. *"The animals trust me. The streams carry my name in whispers, and the winds scatter it across mountains. I've stood against the darkness in forms most folks can't imagine, let alone believe. Each time, I've returned to the stillness of the wild, watching, waiting, ready to rise again when I'm needed."*

He shifted slightly, the firelight catching the scarred edges of his frame. *"This land is more than trees and dirt, more than beasts and men. It's a living, breathing thing, and I'm its keeper. Not because I was asked, but because I was made for it."*

Koda leaned forward, his glowing eyes meeting the flickering flames as if speaking directly to the fire itself. *"And if you're quiet enough, if you listen close, you'll hear the forest call my name too: Koda."*

The campfire crackled softly, its flames lower now, as if humbled by the presence of the one who spoke. The forest seemed to breathe with him, each gust of wind a sigh of relief that its keeper still walked among its shadows.

Koda leaned back into the darkness, his form melding with the shadows of the trees. His voice was softer now, a whisper that carried with the wind.

"The troubles come and go," he said. *"The balance shifts, and I shift with it. But this land... this land remains. And so do I."*

The fire flickered once, a final burst of light before settling into glowing embers. By the time the flames had faded, Koda was gone, leaving nothing but the silence of the forest and the faint scent of pine on the cool mountain air.

Chapter One:

The fire crackled low, its embers glowing like dying stars scattered across the darkened earth. Smoke curled lazily upward, threading itself through the ancient pines that stretched endlessly into the night sky. The forest held its breath, as it often did when Koda sat by the flames. He didn't light fires often—he didn't need to—but tonight was different. Tonight, the forest whispered of a storm approaching, and it wasn't one made of wind or rain.

Koda shifted slightly, his massive form casting long shadows against the surrounding trees. His eyes—dark as the deepest caves and glinting with the wisdom of countless years—watched the fire with an intensity that belied his stillness. Around him, the night pulsed with life. An owl hooted softly, its call answered by the distant rustle of leaves. Somewhere far off, a stream gurgled as it wound its way through the undergrowth, carrying whispers of the forest's secrets.

He drew in a breath, the air heavy with the scent of pine, damp earth, and the faint metallic tang of something unnatural—something wrong. It wasn't the first time he'd caught that scent in recent days, and it wouldn't be the last. But before he could confront what was coming, he needed to ground himself, to remember. Stories had a way of doing that, and Koda had plenty of them.

The fire popped, and Koda's voice rumbled like distant thunder, low and deliberate. *"Do you know what happens when a shadow crosses a clearing in the daylight?"*

He paused, as if expecting an answer, though he was alone. The forest, however, seemed to lean closer, its countless unseen inhabitants hanging on his words.

"They see you," he continued, his tone laced with something that might have been regret. *"Even when they don't understand what they're looking at. Even when they tell themselves it's nothing more than a trick of the light, or a story they'll laugh about later. They see."*

He leaned forward, the firelight dancing across his face. *"It was a long time ago, but I remember it like it happened yesterday. The first time anyone ever saw me and lived to tell about it."*

"It was mid-autumn," Koda began, his voice a rich blend of nostalgia and weariness. *"The leaves had turned, the air crisp enough to carry the faintest sound for miles. I was heading north, following the calls of the geese overhead. I don't usually take the open trails, but that day... well, something told me to step out of the shadows. Maybe I was tired of being unseen. Maybe I wanted to feel the sun on my back. Or maybe, just maybe, the forest wanted me to be seen."*

The fire snapped as he spoke, punctuating his words. *"The clearing was wide, its edges framed by ancient trees that had watched over it for centuries. I stepped into the light, my shadow stretching long across the grass. That's when I smelled them—men."*

Koda's lips curled slightly, not in anger but in a memory of surprise. *"Two of them. They were standing on the far side, one holding a strange device—a camera, though I didn't know the word for it then. The other whispered, his voice trembling like the leaves around him. I could hear their hearts, fast and sharp, like birds trapped in a cage. They didn't move. Just stared."*

He let the moment hang, his gaze fixed on the fire as though he were still standing in that clearing. *"I could've vanished then, melted back into the trees before they had time to blink. But I didn't. Maybe I wanted them to see. Not all of me, just enough to remind them that this world still holds mysteries they can't explain."*

Koda leaned back, his massive hands resting on his knees. *"And so they did. They captured me—not with traps or weapons, but with that device. And they carried that image back to their kind, spreading stories and debates that would echo for years. But they didn't really see me. Not all of me. They saw what they needed to—a monster, a myth, a moment. Nothing more."*

He exhaled, the sound deep and steady. *"That day, I became more than just a whisper in the woods. I became a question. A legend. But legends are a dangerous thing. They make people curious. And curiosity... well, that brings trouble."*

The fire had burned lower now, its light casting flickering shadows across Koda's solemn face. The forest seemed to stir uneasily, as if responding to his words. He tilted his head slightly, listening to a sound only he could hear.

"They're here," he said softly, his voice as much a growl as a whisper. *"Not the men with their cameras. Something worse."*

He stood, his towering form blotting out the firelight. The earth beneath his feet seemed to shift slightly, as though acknowledging his weight, his presence. He reached down and picked up a fallen branch, thick and gnarled, easily the size of a small tree. He tested its weight, then planted it firmly in the ground beside him, like a staff.

"*They don't belong here,*" he murmured, his tone more to himself than the forest. "*The wolves that walk on two legs. They bring death, not balance.*"

He turned his gaze to the darkness beyond the firelight, where the trees stood silent and unmoving. "*The forest warned me. The animals flee. The streams run faster, as though trying to escape. And the scent... that metallic tang. It's the mark of the unnatural.*"

Koda began to walk, his steps silent despite his size. The fire behind him flickered and died, leaving only the faint glow of the moon to light his path. The forest seemed to part for him, its branches whispering in languages older than words.

Koda moved through the forest as if he were part of it, his massive frame weaving silently between the trees. Every step was deliberate, every breath in sync with the rhythm of the wild around him. The moonlight dappled his fur in silver streaks, making him seem even more ethereal—a creature of legend, but undeniably real.

The metallic tang in the air grew stronger, mingling with the earthy scent of damp leaves and pine. Koda's brow furrowed, his keen senses picking up the faintest traces of movement ahead. A broken branch, the whisper of fur brushing against bark—subtle signs that would be missed by anyone less attuned to the forest's language.

"*They're testing the boundaries,*" he muttered, his voice a low rumble that seemed to vibrate the air around him. "*Pushing to see what will break.*"

His grip tightened on the branch he carried, now serving as a makeshift club. It wasn't the first time he'd confronted something that didn't belong, but this felt different. These weren't mere predators or invasive creatures. This was a force driven by hunger and malice, a corruption of the natural order.

The forest opened up into another clearing, smaller this time, the ground littered with the remains of a recent kill. A deer, its body torn apart with a ferocity that spoke of more than hunger. The air was thick with the scent of blood, and Koda knelt beside the carcass, studying it.

The wounds were deep and jagged, the marks of claws that tore not for survival but for pleasure. Koda's lips pressed into a grim line as he traced the marks with one massive finger. His eyes narrowed as he noted the unnatural spacing of the tracks around the body—too large for a wolf, too wide for a bear.

"Werewolves," he said aloud, the word carrying weight as though it had been pulled from the earth itself.

He stood, the branch now resting on his shoulder like an ax. His gaze swept the clearing, catching the faintest glimmer of eyes reflecting the moonlight at the edge of the treeline. They were watching him, testing his resolve. A low growl rumbled from his chest, more warning than challenge. The eyes vanished, melting back into the shadows.

"You've taken your first step too far," he said quietly, his voice carrying a mixture of sorrow and resolve. *"And now, I'll show you the second step is always your last."*

As Koda pressed deeper into the forest, his mind drifted to the stories he'd heard over the centuries. Stories of creatures like the ones he now hunted.

"They called them skinwalkers once," he murmured to himself. *"Others named them moonbeasts, cursed men, the forsaken."* His voice softened as he remembered the elders of a long-vanished tribe, their voices thick with reverence and fear. *"They said the*

moon's light showed them their true nature, and they were cursed to walk in that truth."

He had always been skeptical of such tales. Curses were for men who needed explanations for things they couldn't understand. But what Koda had seen, what he had fought—there was no mistaking the malice in these creatures. They weren't born of nature; they were twisted by something far older, far darker.

Koda's steps slowed as he reached a familiar glade, its ancient trees standing like sentinels. This place had been a sanctuary for him once, a place to rest and heal. Now, it felt different. The air was heavy, the stillness unnatural.

He crouched, his massive hand brushing the ground. The soil was disturbed, claw marks gouging deep into the earth. He could almost feel the echo of the violence that had taken place here. The forest mourned the intrusion, its harmony shattered.

"You don't belong," Koda whispered, his voice low but filled with conviction. *"And I'll make sure you never do."*

The first howl came as he crossed a shallow stream, the sound slicing through the stillness like a blade. It was distant but unmistakable, a call that sent the smaller creatures of the forest into a frenzy of movement. Koda straightened, his grip tightening on the branch.

A second howl answered, closer this time. It carried a different tone, more guttural, more... human. Koda's jaw clenched as he stepped onto the bank, his eyes scanning the darkness.

"You're brave," he muttered, the faintest trace of a smile tugging at the corner of his lips. *"Or foolish."*

The lone wolf stepped into view moments later, its massive form illuminated by a break in the canopy. It moved on two legs, its body hunched but powerful, muscles rippling beneath matted fur. Its eyes glowed with a malevolent intelligence, and its lips curled back to reveal jagged teeth stained with blood.

Koda held his ground, his massive frame radiating calm despite the tension in the air. The werewolf snarled, saliva dripping from its jaws as it crouched, preparing to leap.

"Come on, then," Koda said, his voice steady and low. *"Let's get this over with."*

The werewolf lunged, and Koda swung the branch with the force of a falling tree. The impact sent the creature sprawling, but it recovered quickly, its claws raking through the air as it charged again. Koda sidestepped, his movements surprisingly agile for his size, and brought the branch down hard on the werewolf's back. Bones cracked, and the creature let out a pained howl.

But it didn't stop. It twisted, its claws slashing across Koda's arm, drawing blood. Koda grunted, his grip tightening on the branch as he swung again, this time connecting with the werewolf's jaw. The creature collapsed, its body twitching as it tried to rise.

Koda stepped forward, his massive hand wrapping around the werewolf's throat. He lifted it effortlessly, his eyes locking onto its glowing gaze.

"Your kind doesn't know when to stop," he said, his voice filled with quiet fury. *"But I do."*

With a final, crushing motion, Koda slammed the creature into the ground, its body going limp. He stared at it for a moment, blood dripping from his arm and pooling at his feet.

"This is just the beginning," he said softly, his gaze shifting to the shadows where he knew others were watching. *"You'll come for me now. All of you. And I'll be ready."*

Koda stood over the lifeless body of the werewolf, his breath misting in the cold night air. He crouched down, his massive hand pressing against the earth near the creature's body. The forest was unnervingly quiet now, the usual symphony of crickets and distant owls replaced by an almost suffocating silence. It wasn't just fear that kept the forest still—it was anticipation.

"You've upset the balance," Koda murmured, his voice like a low rumble of thunder. *"And now the forest waits to see if I can restore it."*

The scent of the werewolf's blood was heavy, metallic and acrid, tainting the pure, clean air. Koda's keen senses picked up the faint traces of others. They weren't close yet, but they were moving. The pack would know one of their own had fallen, and they would come.

He reached down and gripped the werewolf's arm, easily lifting its body. It was massive by human standards, but to Koda, it felt like carrying a young deer. He strode to the edge of the clearing and hoisted the body onto the low branch of an ancient tree, letting it hang like a grim warning.

"The pack will find you here," he said, his tone quiet but firm. *"Let them see what happens when they step out of line."*

Koda turned and walked back into the shadows of the forest, the soft thud of his steps absorbed by the earth. As he moved, the forest seemed to breathe again, the rustling leaves and faint calls of animals returning cautiously to life. The message had been sent, and now, Koda would prepare for what came next.

The path ahead twisted through a dense thicket, the branches clawing at Koda's fur as he passed. He paid them no mind, his thoughts drifting to the stories that had brought him to this moment.

He remembered the tales of the first werewolves told to him by an elder of the Lakota, a man whose eyes had seen the birth and death of generations. The elder had spoken of cursed warriors, men who had been granted power by the moon itself but at a terrible cost.

"They were once protectors," the elder had said, his voice crackling like firewood. "Men chosen to guard the sacred places. But power is a dangerous gift. They became beasts, their hearts consumed by hunger. They forgot what they were meant to protect and became the very thing they swore to destroy."

Koda's jaw tightened as he recalled those words. He'd seen it himself, the way power corrupted. These werewolves were no longer the guardians they were once meant to be. They had become predators, threats to the balance he was sworn to protect.

He paused at the edge of a stream, the water sparkling faintly in the moonlight. Kneeling, he dipped his hands into the icy flow, letting the cold bite into his wounds. The blood from his arm stained the water briefly before being carried away, a fleeting reminder of the fight to come.

"Power is nothing without purpose," Koda said to the stream, as if it might carry his words to the forest itself. *"And they've forgotten theirs."*

The hours stretched on as Koda moved deeper into the wilderness. The moon hung high, casting its pale light over the treetops. He could feel the pack closing in, their movements subtle but unmistakable. They were hunting him now, but Koda wasn't prey.

He stopped in a small clearing surrounded by towering pines. The ground here was uneven, littered with broken branches and jagged stones. A place of chaos, but also one of opportunity. Koda scanned the area, his mind calculating the possibilities.

He gripped a fallen log, easily the length of a small car, and hefted it onto one shoulder. Testing its weight, he nodded to himself. *"This will do."*

With deliberate precision, Koda began setting the stage. He dragged the log to the center of the clearing, planting it firmly into the ground to create a makeshift barrier. Nearby, he found a cluster of boulders, each one large enough to crush a man. One by one, he rolled them into position, creating a landscape of obstacles and weapons.

The work was slow, but Koda wasn't in a hurry. He knew the pack would come, and when they did, they would find a battleground ready to greet them. As he worked, he spoke softly, the words more for himself than the forest.

"I've faced worse than you," he said, his tone calm but laced with a quiet fury. *"And they've all learned the same lesson: the forest protects its own."*

As dawn began to creep over the horizon, the forest's whispers grew louder. The pack was close now, their presence a ripple in the air, a vibration that Koda could feel in his bones. He crouched at the edge of the clearing, his massive form hidden among the shadows.

The first werewolf appeared just as the sun began to rise, its hulking silhouette cutting through the dim light. It moved cautiously, its glowing eyes scanning the clearing. Behind it, others emerged, their movements eerily synchronized. They were lean, powerful, and brimming with primal aggression.

But the alpha was not among them.

Koda's eyes narrowed as he watched the werewolves spread out, their claws scraping against the ground as they sniffed the air. They were searching for him, but he would not make it easy.

He gripped the trunk of the log he had positioned earlier, his muscles tensing as he prepared to strike. The forest seemed to hold its breath once more, the tension thick enough to cut with a blade.

The first werewolf stepped closer, its nose twitching as it caught his scent. Koda waited, his grip tightening, his eyes locked on his target. And then, with a roar that shook the trees, he charged.

The log swung through the air with devastating force, connecting with the werewolf's chest and sending it flying into the trunk of a nearby tree. The sound of breaking bones echoed through the clearing as the battle began in earnest.

Koda's roar echoed through the clearing as the massive log in his hands splintered against the werewolf's chest. The creature crumpled to the ground, its body twitching as it tried to rise. Another werewolf lunged from the shadows, its claws slashing through the air, but Koda was ready.

He turned, swinging the jagged remnants of the log like a club. The impact shattered the werewolf's jaw, sending teeth flying as it collapsed in a heap. Koda didn't pause. He planted a massive foot on the chest of the first creature, his weight pinning it down as he brought the log down in a brutal arc. Blood sprayed across the clearing, and the werewolf's struggles ceased.

Two more emerged from the treeline, their growls low and menacing. Koda could see the hesitation in their movements. They weren't mindless beasts; they understood what they were facing. But the pack instinct drove them forward.

The first circled to his left, feinting with sharp, quick movements. The second came straight on, its claws aimed at Koda's throat. He ducked, grabbing the creature by the arm and twisting it with a sickening crack. The werewolf howled in pain, its other arm flailing wildly, but Koda used its own momentum to slam it into the ground.

The second werewolf seized the opportunity, leaping onto Koda's back. Its claws dug into his shoulders, drawing thick lines of blood. Koda grunted, his massive hand reaching up to grab the creature by the scruff of its neck. With a roar, he yanked it off and hurled it into a nearby tree. The force of the impact snapped the trunk, sending the werewolf tumbling to the forest floor.

Koda stepped forward, his footfalls heavy and deliberate. The injured werewolf tried to crawl away, its movements sluggish and desperate. Koda grabbed it by the leg, lifting it effortlessly into the air. For a moment, he stared into its glowing eyes, his expression unreadable.

"This is what happens," he said, his voice low and steady, *"when you forget the rules."*

With a savage motion, he swung the werewolf against the broken tree, its back bending unnaturally as bones shattered. The creature went limp, its body hanging awkwardly over the jagged stump.

Koda didn't have time to savor the brief silence. From the shadows, three more werewolves charged as one, their coordination unnerving in its precision. Koda barely had time to brace himself before the first collided with him, its claws raking across his chest. He staggered but didn't fall, his massive frame absorbing the impact.

The second werewolf came from the side, its jaws snapping at Koda's arm. He swung his fist, the force of the blow knocking the creature to the ground. The third leapt for his throat, but Koda caught it mid-air, his hands closing around its ribcage. With a roar, he squeezed, the sound of cracking bones mingling with the creature's pained howls.

The other two werewolves regrouped, their growls filling the clearing. Koda dropped the shattered body of the third and turned to face them, his chest heaving but his resolve unshaken.

"You're persistent," he said, wiping blood from his brow. *"I'll give you that."*

One of the werewolves lunged, but this time Koda was ready. He sidestepped, grabbing a boulder he had positioned earlier. With a grunt of effort, he lifted it over his head and brought it crashing down onto the werewolf's skull. The ground shook with the impact, and the creature lay still.

The last werewolf hesitated, its glowing eyes darting between Koda and its fallen packmates. Koda took a step forward, his presence overwhelming, his gaze unyielding.

"Go on," he said, his voice a growl. "Run. Tell your alpha what happened here."

The werewolf snarled but took a step back. Then another. With a final growl of frustration, it turned and bolted into the forest, its howls fading into the distance.

Koda stood in the aftermath of the battle, his massive frame illuminated by the faint light of dawn breaking through the trees. The clearing was a mess of blood, broken branches, and shattered bodies. His own wounds stung, the deep gashes on his arms and chest reminding him of the price of his victory.

He knelt beside one of the fallen werewolves, his massive hand resting briefly on its head. For all their ferocity, these creatures weren't mindless. They were victims of something older and darker, a curse that twisted them into monsters.

"I didn't ask for this," he said softly, his voice heavy with sorrow. *"But it's my burden to carry."*

He rose, his eyes scanning the treeline. The pack wasn't finished. The alpha would come, and it wouldn't come alone. But Koda wasn't afraid. He had faced worse, and he would face worse again. It was his role, his purpose. He was the balance, the line that no one crossed without consequence.

With one last look at the carnage, Koda turned and walked into the forest, his steps slow but steady. The battle had been won, but the war was far from over.

Chapter Two:

THE FOREST WHISPERED its secrets in the language of rustling leaves and shifting shadows, but tonight, its voice trembled. Koda moved through the ancient woods with the deliberate steps of someone who had walked this path a thousand times, yet tonight it felt foreign, wrong. The metallic tang of blood still lingered faintly in the air, a reminder of the lone werewolf he had dispatched. But it wasn't just the scent that clung to him; it was the knowledge of what lay ahead.

"They were always wolves," Koda murmured, his voice breaking the quiet like a low roll of thunder. *"Before the moon took hold of them. Before their hunger became something else."*

He stopped, his eyes scanning the treetops where the moon hung like a pale specter. The stories of the werewolves were as old as the forest itself, whispered around campfires and carved into the memories of the people who once thrived here. Koda had seen those people, lived alongside them, and learned their ways. He carried their stories now, just as the trees carried the weight of the wind.

The Lakota elders had called them the Forsaken, men who had turned their backs on the balance of life in pursuit of power. Koda could still hear the voice of the shaman who first told him the tale, a voice rich with age and reverence for the natural world.

"They were warriors once," the shaman had said, his eye distant as he gazed into the fire. "Chosen by the spirits of the hunt, bound to the moon's cycles. But they were not content with what was given. They wanted more. Strength beyond strength, speed beyond the wind, hunger that could never be satisfied."

Koda had listened in silence as the shaman described how the warriors had sought the moon's favor, performing rituals that broke the sacred bonds with the land. Their prayers were answered, but not in the way they hoped. The moon granted them its light, but it also gave them its shadow—a curse that turned their bodies into beasts and their hearts into voids.

"They became the Forsaken," the shaman had continued, his voice heavy with sorrow. "Hunters who no longer hunted for sustenance, but for the thrill of the kill. Their howls were once a song of unity; now they are a cry of despair. They forgot who they were. And so, they became what they feared."

The memory of the shaman's words faded as Koda knelt by a stream, his massive hands brushing the surface of the water. The current was sluggish, its usual clarity clouded with silt and an unnatural darkness. He frowned, dipping his hand deeper into the water, feeling its chill.

"They've been here," he said softly, the weight of his words sinking into the forest around him.

He stood, his eyes following the stream as it wound its way through the trees. The water seemed to struggle against an invisible force, its flow disrupted by the presence of something unnatural. Koda's gaze narrowed as he spotted faint claw marks on a tree trunk nearby, their grooves deep and deliberate.

"Marking their territory," he muttered, his voice tinged with quiet anger. *"But this isn't theirs."*

The forest was alive with tension. Birds that should have been singing at dawn were silent. Small animals that would normally dart through the underbrush were nowhere to be seen. Even the wind seemed to hold its breath, as if afraid to disturb the growing unease.

Koda followed the stream until it opened into a small clearing. The ground here was torn, the grass flattened and stained with blood. In the center lay the remains of a campsite—torn tents, scattered belongings, and a fire pit long extinguished. The metallic scent was stronger here, mingling with the unmistakable stench of fear.

Koda crouched beside the remnants of a tent, his fingers brushing against a scrap of fabric. It was damp with dew and something darker. He sniffed the air, his sharp senses picking up faint traces of human sweat and terror. Whoever had been here hadn't stood a chance.

He moved to the center of the campsite, where a small totem had been erected—a crude figure made of twigs and bones, bound together with strips of hide. It stood barely a foot tall, but its presence was overwhelming. Koda recognized it immediately.

"A warning," he said, his voice heavy. *"Or an invitation."*

The totem was an old trick, one used by the Forsaken to stake their claim and intimidate those who ventured too close. It wasn't just a marker; it was a challenge. The message was clear: this is our land now.

Koda reached out and gripped the totem in one massive hand. The bones crumbled easily under his grip, the twigs snapping with a brittle finality. He tossed the remains aside and stood, his eyes scanning the edge of the clearing.

"If you want to claim it," he said, his voice rising into the stillness, *"then come take it."*

The response was immediate. A howl tore through the forest, low and guttural, echoing off the trees like a warning shot. It was answered by another, then another, the voices overlapping until the air vibrated with their intensity.

"They're close," Koda said, his tone calm despite the growing tension. *"Too close."*

He turned back toward the stream, moving with purpose. The forest seemed to shift around him, its ancient roots and branches bending slightly as if to guide his path. He didn't need to see the pack to know they were watching. He could feel their eyes, their hunger.

The howls grew louder, weaving through the forest like a hunting song. Koda's steps quickened, his massive form disappearing into the shadows as the pack's chorus reached its peak. They were coming, and Koda knew this was only the beginning.

Chapter Three:

THE FOREST HAD GROWN quieter as the night deepened, but it wasn't the kind of quiet that brought peace. This was the silence of a predator stalking its prey, the stillness of something waiting to pounce. Koda moved through the shadows with practiced ease, his massive frame at odds with his almost silent steps. The trees loomed like silent witnesses, their branches twisted into skeletal shapes under the pale light of the moon.

He paused at a small ridge, his eyes scanning the valley below. The faint glimmer of a stream cut through the underbrush, its waters moving sluggishly as though burdened by the weight of what had passed here. Koda crouched, his senses sharp, his breath slow and steady.

"They're watching," he murmured, his voice barely louder than the rustle of leaves. *"But they're not ready yet."*

The faintest sound reached him—a crack of a branch, the rustle of leaves disturbed by something heavy. Koda's gaze snapped to the source, his eyes narrowing. He didn't move, his massive form blending seamlessly with the shadows. Whatever it was, it was circling him, testing his awareness.

"They want to know what I am," he muttered. *"Let's show them."*

The attack came suddenly. A blur of fur and muscle burst from the underbrush, claws outstretched and teeth bared. Koda moved faster than seemed possible for his size, sidestepping the attack and swinging his arm in a wide arc. His fist connected with the creature's side, the impact sending it sprawling into the dirt.

The werewolf was smaller than the one he'd fought before, but its movements were faster, more deliberate. It rolled to its feet in a fluid motion, crouching low as it bared its fangs. Its eyes glowed a sickly yellow, full of intelligence and malice.

Koda straightened, his towering form dwarfing the creature. He didn't speak, his presence alone enough to carry the weight of his challenge. The werewolf snarled, saliva dripping from its maw as it lunged again. This time, Koda didn't dodge.

He caught the creature mid-leap, his massive hands wrapping around its torso. The werewolf thrashed violently, its claws raking against Koda's arms, but he held firm. With a guttural growl, he slammed the creature into the ground, the force of the impact shaking the earth beneath them. The werewolf howled in pain but didn't stop struggling.

"You don't give up easily," Koda said, his voice a low growl. *"Good. Neither do I."*

With a single motion, he hoisted the creature into the air and hurled it against a nearby tree. The trunk cracked under the force, splinters flying as the werewolf crumpled to the ground. It tried to rise, its movements sluggish and pained, but Koda was already on it.

The werewolf twisted as Koda reached for it, its claws flashing in the moonlight. It slashed at his face, leaving a shallow cut along his jaw. Koda grunted, more annoyed than hurt, and retaliated with a powerful backhand that sent the creature tumbling once more.

"You're not just testing me," he said, his tone thoughtful even in the heat of battle. *"You're learning. Your alpha sent you for more than a fight."*

The werewolf snarled, circling him now, its movements slower but no less dangerous. Koda crouched slightly, his massive hands flexing as he prepared for the next attack. He could feel the creature's desperation, its need to prove itself—or die trying.

The werewolf lunged again, this time aiming low. Koda shifted his weight, letting the creature's momentum carry it past him. As it landed, he grabbed it by the leg and swung it like a rag doll, slamming it into the ground with enough force to crack the earth beneath them. The werewolf howled, its voice sharp and piercing, but Koda didn't relent.

With a savage motion, he gripped its jaws and twisted. The werewolf's body went limp, its glowing eyes fading as silence fell over the clearing.

Koda stood over the lifeless body, his chest heaving as he wiped blood from his brow. The fight had been brutal, but it wasn't the victory that concerned him. It was the purpose. This wasn't a random attack. The werewolf had been sent—deliberate, calculated, and cruel.

"They're not just hunting me," he said aloud, his voice carrying into the stillness. *"They're testing me. Measuring my strength."*

He knelt beside the body, studying it closely. The creature was lean and muscular, its fur matted with blood and dirt. On its chest, faint scars formed a pattern—a symbol. Koda traced it with one massive finger, his expression darkening.

"This isn't natural," he muttered. *"Your alpha did this to you."*

The symbol was old, older than the forest itself. It carried a weight that Koda recognized but couldn't fully place. He rose, his gaze sweeping the treetops where the first hints of dawn were beginning to appear.

"If you think this will scare me," he said, his tone steady and resolute, *"you don't know what you've woken up."*

He hoisted the werewolf's body and carried it to the edge of the clearing. With a single motion, he draped it over the low branch of an ancient tree, its lifeless form hanging as a grim warning.

"Come find me," he said, his voice low but carrying. *"Let's end this."*

As Koda moved deeper into the forest, the howls began again. This time, they were different—shorter, sharper, and more frenzied. The pack had found their fallen comrade, and their response was immediate.

"They'll come now," Koda said, his tone calm despite the rising tension. *"All of them."*

He quickened his pace, his massive strides carrying him through the forest with ease. The terrain grew rougher, the trees thicker, but Koda moved as though the land itself welcomed him. He could feel the pack closing in, their presence a ripple in the air that set his senses on edge.

The howls were joined by a new sound—a low, resonant growl that seemed to vibrate the very ground. Koda stopped, his head tilting slightly as he listened. It wasn't just a growl; it was a voice, deep and commanding, filled with malice.

The alpha was calling.

Koda's lips pressed into a grim line as he continued forward. The forest seemed to shift around him, its shadows deepening its silence growing heavier. The alpha's call was a challenge, a promise of what was to come.

"They think they're ready," Koda said, his voice carrying a hint of both weariness and resolve. *"But so am I."*

Chapter Four:

THE FOREST FELT ALIVE with tension, every tree and shadow a potential hiding place for the predators that stalked him. Koda moved cautiously, his massive frame gliding through the underbrush with surprising stealth. The werewolves' howls echoed in the distance, closer now but still faint enough to be searching.

"They'll come fast when they catch my trail," he muttered, his voice low as he scanned the terrain. *"They're testing their limits. Testing mine."*

The moonlight filtered through the trees, illuminating patches of the forest floor. Koda crouched by a cluster of ferns, brushing his massive hand over the soil. The faint impression of clawed paws stood out against the soft earth. He sniffed the air, catching the acrid tang of the pack's scent.

"They're spreading out," he said to himself, rising to his full height. *"Trying to corner me."*

His eyes flicked to the trees above. He knew the pack's strategy. They would push him toward a kill zone, driving him with their numbers and speed. But Koda wasn't prey. He was the forest's keeper, and the forest always had answers.

The first attack came suddenly. A blur of movement from his left, barely visible in the moonlight. Koda turned just in time to raise his arm, catching the werewolf mid-leap. Its claws raked against his forearm, leaving shallow gashes, but Koda's grip was unrelenting.

With a growl, he swung the creature into a nearby tree. The impact shook the ground, and the werewolf crumpled to the forest floor, dazed but not defeated. It rose shakily, its glowing eyes filled with rage, and lunged again.

Koda met the charge head-on, his massive hand closing around the werewolf's throat. He lifted it effortlessly, its legs kicking wildly, and slammed it into the ground. The creature let out a strangled howl before going limp.

"Too eager," Koda said, his voice calm despite the adrenaline coursing through him. He glanced around, his senses attuned to the forest's whispers. The others were close.

The next howl was closer, sharper, and more commanding. Koda turned toward the sound, his eyes narrowing. The pack was no longer testing him—they were hunting in earnest.

He moved swiftly, his steps heavy but deliberate, each one carrying him deeper into the forest. The trees closed in around him, their branches forming a dense canopy that blocked out the moonlight. The darkness was his ally now, and Koda used it to his advantage.

Behind him, the howls grew louder. He could hear the pack moving through the underbrush, their claws scraping against roots and rocks. They were fast—faster than any natural predator—but Koda knew these woods better than they did.

He reached a narrow ravine, its rocky walls descending into a shallow creek. Without hesitation, Koda jumped, landing with a heavy thud that echoed through the gorge. He crouched low, his eyes scanning the edges of the ravine as he moved along the creek bed.

The first werewolf appeared moments later, its glowing eyes peering over the edge. It sniffed the air, its lips curling into a snarl as it caught his scent. A second joined it, then a third. They were closing in, their snarls blending into a symphony of hunger and aggression.

Koda paused, his gaze falling on a cluster of loose boulders at the base of the ravine. The pack was descending now, their claws finding purchase on the rocky walls as they approached.

"Let's see how well you climb," he muttered, planting his massive hands against one of the larger rocks. With a grunt of effort, he heaved it upward, the boulder rolling free from its resting place and crashing into the ravine below.

The first werewolf yelped in surprise as the boulder struck it, sending it tumbling back down the rocky slope. The second narrowly dodged the cascade of rocks that followed, its growls turning to panicked snarls as it scrambled for cover.

Koda didn't stop. He grabbed another boulder, then another, using his immense strength to send them tumbling toward his pursuers. The ravine filled with the sounds of crashing rocks and the howls of wounded werewolves.

When the dust settled, Koda stood at the center of the creek bed, his chest heaving. The pack had retreated for now, their injured comrades dragging themselves back into the shadows.

"That's one lesson," Koda said, his voice low but firm. *"Don't try to corner me."*

The forest fell silent again, but Koda knew better than to think the hunt was over. The pack would regroup, their alpha driving them forward with relentless precision. Koda's own injuries, though minor, were beginning to weigh on him. The gashes on his arm stung with every movement, and his muscle ached from the effort of the fight.

He climbed out of the ravine, his massive hands gripping roots and rocks as he pulled himself upward. The moon had shifted higher in the sky, its pale light casting long shadows over the forest.

As he reached the top, he paused, his eyes scanning the horizon. The howls had stopped, replaced by an eerie stillness. It wasn't fear that kept the pack quiet—it was strategy.

"They're smarter than I thought," Koda muttered, wiping blood from his brow. *"Good. It'll make this more interesting."*

The next attack came with no warning. Three werewolves burst from the shadows, their glowing eyes and snarling jaws filling Koda's vision. He reacted instinctively, swinging a massive branch he had picked up along the way. The first werewolf took the full force of the blow, its body crumpling as it was sent flying into a tree.

The second and third came at him together, their claws raking at his chest and shoulders. Koda roared, his voice a primal sound that shook the forest. He grabbed one by the arm and twisted, the sickening snap of bone followed by a howl of pain.

The third creature leapt onto his back, its jaws snapping at his neck. Koda staggered but didn't fall. Instead, he reached over his shoulder, gripping the werewolf by the scruff of its neck and pulling it free. With a savage motion, he hurled it to the ground and stomped down with all his weight.

The clearing was a chaos of snarls and growls, blood and broken bodies littering the ground. Koda stood at the center, his massive frame heaving with each breath.

As the last of the werewolves retreated into the forest, dragging their wounded with them, Koda remained still. His fur was matted with blood—his and theirs—and his muscles ached with the effort of the fight.

"They're not done," he said quietly, his gaze fixed on the darkness beyond the trees. *"But neither am I."*

He crouched by a small stream, washing the blood from his hands and face. The water was cold and soothing, its touch a reminder of the balance he was fighting to protect.

"The alpha's waiting," Koda said, his voice steady. *"He thinks he can wear me down. But he doesn't understand. The forest doesn't give up. And neither do I."*

Chapter Five:

The forest had fallen into a silence so deep it felt oppressive, as if even the trees were holding their breath. Koda stood at the base of a hill, his chest rising and falling steadily as he scanned the darkness. The pack's howls had ceased hours ago, replaced by an unsettling stillness.

"They're waiting," he muttered, his voice low. *"Not for me. For him."*

He could feel it—a presence on the edge of his senses, stronger and darker than the others. The alpha was near. Koda didn't know if it was the moon or something else, but this creature carried an aura that rippled through the forest like a storm about to break.

Koda moved uphill, his massive feet pressing into the earth. The incline was steep, the terrain rough, but he didn't hesitate. His instincts pulled him forward, a primal certainty guiding his steps.

At the summit, the forest opened into a wide plateau. The moon hung low over the clearing, its pale light casting long shadows across the uneven ground. In the center stood a massive figure, its fur black as midnight, its eyes burning like molten gold. The alpha.

The alpha didn't move as Koda stepped into the clearing. It stood perfectly still, its gaze fixed on him with a terrifying intensity. This was no ordinary werewolf. Its sheer size rivaled Koda's, and its stance radiated power and control.

Koda stopped a dozen paces away, his broad shoulders squared. He could feel the alpha's dominance, an unspoken challenge that hung heavy in the air. For a moment, neither moved, the silence stretching between them like a taut wire.

"*You're the one,*" Koda said finally, his voice calm but firm. "*The one they follow.*"

The alpha's lips curled back, revealing jagged teeth. It let out a low growl, a sound that vibrated through the ground beneath Koda's feet. The message was clear: this was its territory, and Koda was an intruder.

"*You think this forest belongs to you?*" Koda asked, his tone unyielding. "*You're wrong.*"

The alpha crouched, its claws digging into the dirt. It didn't speak—not in words—but its movements carried meaning. It wasn't here to argue. It was here to fight.

The alpha moved with blinding speed, its massive frame a blur as it closed the distance between them. Koda barely had time to react before the creature was upon him, its claws slashing toward his chest. He stepped back, the swipe missing by inches, and countered with a powerful swing of his arm.

The impact was like thunder, Koda's fist connecting with the alpha's jaw. The creature staggered but didn't fall. Instead, it lunged again, its jaws snapping at Koda's shoulder. This time, it struck true, its teeth sinking into his flesh.

Koda roared, a sound that echoed through the forest. He grabbed the alpha by the scruff of its neck and wrenched it free, blood dripping from the wound. With a savage motion, he hurled the creature to the ground, the earth shaking with the force of the impact.

The alpha rolled to its feet, unfazed by the blow. It circled Koda now, its movements deliberate and predatory. Koda watched it carefully, his own movements measured. This wasn't a mindless beast—it was a calculating predator.

The first howl broke through the night, followed by another, then another. Koda's eyes flicked to the edge of the clearing, where the pack began to emerge. They didn't charge. They didn't move. They simply watched, their glowing eyes fixed on the battle.

"They're waiting for you to win," Koda said, his gaze snapping back to the alpha. *"Or die."*

The alpha snarled, its muscles coiling as it prepared to strike again. This time, the attack was faster, more vicious. The alpha's claws raked across Koda's chest, leaving deep gashes that burned with pain. Koda staggered, his massive hand pressing against the wound as blood seeped between his fingers.

The alpha pressed its advantage, lunging again. Koda caught it mid-air, his hands closing around its torso. With a roar, he slammed the creature into the ground, the impact cracking the earth beneath them. But the alpha twisted, its claws catching Koda's side as it broke free.

The pack howled again, their voices rising in unison. Koda glanced at them, their presence a reminder of the stakes. If he fell, the forest would fall with him.

Koda took a step back, his massive frame heaving with exertion. The alpha growled, its eyes locked onto him as it crouched for another attack. But this time, Koda didn't wait.

He grabbed a massive branch that had fallen nearby, hefting it like a club. The alpha charged, and Koda swung with all his might. The branch connected with the creature's side, splintering on impact and sending the alpha tumbling into a tree.

The alpha rose slowly, its movements deliberate. Blood matted its fur, but its eyes burned brighter, its resolve unshaken. Koda took another branch, this one thicker, and swung again. The alpha dodged, its claws flashing as it closed the distance.

The fight became a blur of motion—claws, teeth, fists, and wood colliding in a symphony of violence. Blood stained the ground, the scent of it heavy in the air. Koda's wounds deepened, his strength waning, but he refused to fall.

The alpha snarled, its movements slowing as the fight dragged on. It lunged once more, its claws aiming for Koda's throat, but Koda caught it mid-strike. With a roar, he drove the creature into the ground, pinning it beneath him.

The pack howled, their cries filled with a mix of fear and fury. The alpha growled, its body twisting as it tried to break free, but Koda held firm.

"You've taken enough," Koda said, his voice a low growl. *"This forest isn't yours."*

The alpha snarled one last time before twisting free and retreating into the shadows. The pack followed, their howls fading into the distance. Koda stood alone in the clearing, his chest heaving, his blood staining the earth.

Chapter Six:

KODA LEANED HEAVILY against a tree, his breath ragged and shallow. His wounds throbbed, the deep gashes on his chest and arms leaking blood that glistened in the moonlight. The alpha had left its mark—both physically and in Koda's mind. For the first time in a long while, he felt the ache of vulnerability.

The forest whispered around him, its ancient voice carrying through the rustling leaves and the soft sigh of the wind. It was as though the trees themselves mourned his injuries, their branches bending slightly toward him in quiet solidarity.

"You've seen worse," Koda muttered to himself, his voice a low rumble. *"You've walked away from worse."*

He straightened, his massive frame silhouetted against the pale light filtering through the canopy. The forest stretched out before him, endless and alive, its energy pulsing in time with his own. He had no choice but to keep moving. The pack would not give him the luxury of rest.

The journey was slow and arduous. Each step sent jolts of pain through Koda's body, but he pressed on, guided by the forest's subtle signs. A trail of moss-covered stones led him to a hidden glade, its entrance framed by ancient trees whose roots twisted together like the clasped hands of old friends.

The glade was a place of stillness and peace. A stream bubbled quietly along one edge, its crystal-clear waters reflecting the moonlight. Soft moss carpeted the ground, and the air was thick with the scent of pine and damp earth.

Koda knelt by the stream, his massive hands cupping the cool water. He splashed it over his face and wounds, the icy sting jolting him into focus. The water carried away the blood, leaving faint trails of red that disappeared into the earth.

"This will do," he said quietly, his voice steady despite the exhaustion that weighed on him.

He lowered himself onto the moss, his body sinking into the softness. The forest seemed to sigh in relief, as if grateful that he had found a moment of respite. Above him, the stars glittered like distant fires, their light a reminder of the vastness of the world beyond the trees.

As Koda lay in the glade, his thoughts drifted to the battles he had fought and the role he had played for longer than he could remember. He wasn't just a creature of the forest—he was its keeper, its guardian. It was a role he had never asked for but one he had accepted, nonetheless.

"They don't understand," he murmured, his gaze fixed on the stars. *"The balance isn't something you can see. It's something you feel. Something you keep, no matter the cost."*

His mind wandered to the alpha and the pack. They were more than just predators; they were a disruption, a corruption of the natural order. Their presence wasn't just a threat to the forest—it was a threat to everything Koda stood for.

"I've fought worse," he said, his voice resolute. *"And I've survived."*

The forest seemed to hear his resolve. The wind picked up slightly, carrying the faint scent of herbs and wildflowers. Koda sat up, his sharp eyes catching the glint of something near the stream. He moved toward it slowly, his movements deliberate.

Nestled among the rocks was a cluster of plants, their leaves shimmering faintly in the moonlight. Koda recognized them immediately—healing herbs, rare and powerful, known only to those who listened to the forest's whispers.

"Thank you," he said quietly, his voice filled with genuine gratitude.

He crushed the leaves in his massive hands, their oils releasing a sharp, medicinal scent. He pressed the mixture into his wounds, the sting sharp but cleansing. The herbs worked quickly, their natural magic easing the pain and slowing the bleeding.

The forest had always provided. It was both a home and a partner, its roots and branches intertwined with Koda's very being. He felt its strength seep into him, bolstering his resolve.

The hours passed, and Koda's strength began to return. His wounds, while not fully healed, no longer bled freely. He stood, his massive frame casting a long shadow across the glade.

The pack would come for him again. Of that, he was certain. But this time, he would be ready.

He moved through the glade, gathering what he could. A sturdy branch became a makeshift club, its weight familiar in his hands. Rocks were stacked in strategic places, their sharp edges prepared for the next confrontation. Koda worked methodically, his movements steady and deliberate.

"You think you've broken me," he said, his voice carrying into the stillness. *"You're wrong."*

As dawn approached, the forest began to stir. Birds called softly from the treetops, their songs tentative but hopeful. The wind shifted, carrying a faint but familiar scent. Koda froze, his senses sharp.

"They're close," he said, his voice low.

The pack was on the move again. Their scent was faint but unmistakable, a mix of blood and musk that clung to the air like smoke. Koda hefted his club, his gaze hardening.

"This forest isn't yours," he said, his tone resolute. *"And it never will be."*

Chapter Seven:

THE FOREST PULSED WITH life, but not the kind that brought peace. The usual rhythm—the hum of insects, the rustle of leaves—had been replaced by a primal energy that felt like the land itself was preparing for war. Koda moved through the dense undergrowth, his massive hands brushing past branches and vines, his eyes scanning every shadow.

His wounds throbbed with each step, the deep gashes on his chest and arms still raw despite the forest's gifts. But pain was a familiar companion, one he bore with the stoic resolve of someone who had endured far worse. He wasn't here to rest. He was here to finish what the alpha had started.

Koda crouched by a cluster of rocks, his massive frame hidden in the shadows. The air was heavy with the pack's scent—a mix of musk, blood, and something darker. He could hear them moving, their snarls and growls carried on the wind.

"They think they're the hunters," he muttered, his voice low and steady. *"Let's show them how wrong they are."*

He hefted a large branch, easily the size of a small tree, and planted it upright in the soft earth. Nearby, he arranged a cluster of jagged stones, their sharp edges glinting faintly in the moonlight. Each movement was deliberate, each placement precise. The forest had taught him well; every rock, every tree, every stream could be a weapon if used correctly.

As he worked, his mind drifted to the stories of the first hunters, the men and women who had once walked this land with bows and spears. They had understood the balance of nature, the delicate thread that connected predator and prey. But the werewolves had severed that thread, turning the hunt into something monstrous.

"They forgot the rules," Koda said, his voice a quiet growl. *"Now they'll remember."*

The pack came just before dawn, their glowing eyes piercing the darkness like embers in the night. Koda heard them before he saw them, the faint crunch of leaves underfoot, the soft growl that carried through the air. They moved as one, a coordinated force driven by the alpha's will.

Koda crouched low behind a fallen log, his massive hands gripping a makeshift club—a thick branch reinforced with vines and stones. He watched as the first werewolf entered the clearing, its nose twitching as it sniffed the air.

"You're too eager," Koda muttered.

He waited until the creature was fully in the clearing before striking. With a roar that shook the trees, he swung the club, the force of the blow sending the werewolf flying into a nearby tree. The crack of bone echoed through the clearing as the creature crumpled to the ground.

Two more emerged from the shadows, their snarls filling the air as they charged. Koda met them head-on, his massive frame moving with surprising agility. He caught the first by the arm, twisting until the bone snapped, and hurled it into the second. Both creatures tumbled to the ground in a heap.

"You wanted this fight," Koda said, his voice cold. *"Now you've got it."*

The pack didn't retreat. More werewolves poured into the clearing, their claws flashing in the pale light of dawn. Koda stood his ground, his massive club swinging in wide arcs that broke bones and sent bodies flying. But the pack was relentless, their sheer numbers pressing him back.

Koda's foot caught on a root, and he stumbled. A werewolf seized the opportunity, lunging for his throat. Koda caught it mid-air, his massive hands gripping its jaws. With a savage growl, he tore the creature apart, blood spraying across the clearing as its lifeless halves fell to the ground.

Another leapt at him from behind, its claws raking across his back. Koda roared in pain, spinning and slamming his club into the creature's side. The impact shattered ribs, and the werewolf let out a pained howl before collapsing.

The ground beneath him was slick with blood, the air thick with the metallic tang of violence. But Koda was unyielding. He was the forest's keeper, and this was his domain.

He backed toward a large oak, its massive trunk rising like a sentinel above the carnage. The tree had stood for centuries, its roots anchoring it firmly in the earth. Koda pressed his back against it, using the sturdy trunk as cover as the pack regrouped.

"You want me?" he growled, his voice carrying across the clearing. *"Come and get me."*

The pack hesitated, their growls low and uncertain. Then a new figure emerged from the shadows—a massive werewolf, its size rivaling Koda's. Its fur was darker, its eyes brighter, and its stance radiated authority. This was no ordinary pack member. This was the alpha's lieutenant.

"So, you're the second in command," Koda said, his tone measured. *"Let's see what you've got."*

The lieutenant didn't wait. It charged with a speed and ferocity that took even Koda by surprise. Its claws raked across his chest, tearing through fur and flesh. Koda grunted, the pain sharp and immediate, but he didn't falter.

He swung his club, but the lieutenant ducked, its movements fluid and precise. It lunged again, its jaws snapping at Koda's arm. This time, Koda was ready. He caught the creature by the neck, his massive hands closing around its throat.

"You're fast," he said, his voice a low growl. *"But not fast enough."*

With a roar, Koda slammed the lieutenant into the ground, the impact shaking the earth. The creature twisted free, its claws slashing at Koda's leg. Koda staggered, but he recovered quickly, his club swinging in a wide arc that connected with the lieutenant's side. The werewolf let out a pained howl, but it didn't fall.

The fight was brutal, each blow leaving both combatants bloodied and battered. The clearing became a battlefield, the ground churned into mud by the violence of their clash.

Finally, Koda saw his opening. The lieutenant lunged for his throat, and Koda stepped aside, his massive hand gripping the creature's leg. With a savage motion, he swung it into a nearby tree, the impact snapping the creature's spine. The lieutenant let out one last, gurgling growl before going limp.

The pack watched in silence as their lieutenant fell. Their glowing eyes flicked between Koda and the lifeless body, their growls subdued. For a moment, the forest was still.

Koda stood over the fallen creature, his chest heaving, his fur matted with blood. He dropped his club, the weapon splintered and useless after the fight. He looked at the pack, his gaze unwavering.

"This is your only warning," he said, his voice carrying through the stillness. *"Leave. Now."*

The pack hesitated, their growls low and uncertain. Then, one by one, they retreated into the shadows, their forms disappearing into the forest. Koda watched them go, his massive frame still and unyielding.

As the sun rose, Koda turned back to the clearing. The ground was littered with the bodies of fallen werewolves, their blood soaking into the earth. He knelt beside the lieutenant, his massive hand resting briefly on its head.

"You followed the wrong leader," he said quietly.

He rose and looked toward the horizon, where the forest stretched endlessly. The alpha was still out there, and Koda knew it wouldn't stop until one of them was dead.

"This isn't over," he said, his voice steady. *"Not yet."*

Chapter Eight:

THE FOREST GREW DARKER as Koda moved deeper into the alpha's domain. The trees were older here, their gnarled branches intertwining to form a canopy that blocked out the sky. The air was heavier, damp and tinged with a metallic scent that clung to Koda's senses.

"This place is wrong," he muttered, his voice barely above a growl. *"Even the trees feel it."*

The land sloped downward, the underbrush thinning as the forest gave way to rocky terrain. Ahead, a jagged cave mouth yawned open, its edges marked with clawed symbols that radiated malevolence. Bones littered the ground outside, cracked and scattered like grim offerings.

Koda stopped at the cave's entrance, his massive form framed against the darkness. He could feel the alpha's presence, a pulsing energy that seemed to vibrate through the stone.

"You've made this your home," Koda said, his voice steady. *"Let's see if you're willing to die for it."*

The cave was cold and damp, its walls slick with moisture. The air inside was thick, carrying the stench of decay. Koda moved cautiously, his massive hands brushing against the stone as his eyes adjusted to the darkness.

The first attack came quickly. Two werewolves lunged from the shadows, their snarls echoing off the cavern walls. Koda reacted instinctively, swinging a heavy rock, he had picked up at the entrance. The impact shattered the skull of the first creature, sending it crumpling to the ground.

The second werewolf circled him, its glowing eyes filled with malice. Koda dropped the rock and charged, his massive form barreling into the creature. They collided with the force of a falling tree, Koda's hands closing around its neck. With a sharp twist, he ended its life, its body collapsing in a heap.

"They're defending something," he muttered, stepping over the bodies. *"Or someone."*

As Koda ventured deeper, the walls of the cave began to change. Symbols were etched into the stone, their lines jagged and chaotic. They glowed faintly in the darkness, pulsing with an unnatural energy.

Koda stopped to study one of the markings, his massive hand tracing its grooves. The symbol radiated a cold, malevolent power, one that sent a shiver through even his towering frame.

"This isn't just instinct," he said quietly. *"The alpha isn't just a leader. It's something more."*

The symbols grew denser as he progressed, their glow intensifying. The air became harder to breathe, the oppressive energy pressing against Koda like a physical weight. He clenched his fists, his resolve hardening.

"You've poisoned this place," he growled. *"And now, I'll tear it down."*

The tunnel narrowed, forcing Koda to crouch as he moved forward. The ground was uneven, jagged rocks cutting into his feet with every step. He could hear the faint sound of water dripping, each drop echoing like a drumbeat in the silence.

Suddenly, a growl broke the stillness. Koda froze, his eyes scanning the darkness ahead. A pair of glowing eyes appeared, followed by another, and then another. Three werewolves emerged from the shadows, their movements slow and deliberate.

Koda straightened as much as the tunnel allowed, his massive frame nearly scraping the ceiling. He grabbed a loose stalactite, its sharp tip fitting perfectly in his hand, and waited.

The first werewolf lunged, its claws outstretched. Koda swung the stalactite like a spear, driving it into the creature's chest. It let out a strangled howl before collapsing, its body twitching as it bled out.

The second and third attacked simultaneously, their claws slashing through the air. Koda ducked, the narrow space limiting their movements as much as his. He grabbed one by the arm, twisting until the bone snapped, and hurled it into the other. The impact sent both creatures crashing into the wall, where Koda finished them with a brutal stomp.

The silence returned, broken only by Koda's heavy breathing. He dropped the bloodied stalactite and pressed forward, his resolve unshaken.

The tunnel opened into a massive chamber, its ceiling disappearing into darkness. The air was stifling, the oppressive energy radiating from the walls almost unbearable. In the center of the chamber stood the alpha.

It was larger than before, its fur matted with blood and its eyes glowing like molten gold. The alpha's presence filled the room, a palpable force that seemed to press against Koda's chest.

"You've made this place a tomb," Koda said, his voice steady. *"Let's see who it buries."*

The alpha didn't respond. It didn't need to. Its growl was low and rumbling, a sound that reverberated through the chamber like an earthquake. The pack began to emerge from the shadows, their glowing eyes forming a ring around Koda.

He glanced at them, his massive hands clenching into fists. *"You're too late to save him."*

The alpha lunged, and the battle began.

The fight was brutal, the chamber echoing with the sounds of claws, teeth, and fists. Koda's strength and resolve were matched only by the alpha's ferocity. Each blow sent shockwaves through the cavern, the walls trembling under the strain.

The pack circled but didn't intervene, their loyalty to the alpha overriding their instincts. Koda used the terrain to his advantage, slamming the alpha into the walls and hurling loose rocks at its head. The fight raged on, both combatants bloodied and exhausted.

Finally, Koda saw his opportunity. He grabbed a massive stalagmite, its base cracked and unstable, and heaved with all his strength. The rock broke free, crashing into the alpha and pinning it to the ground.

The cavern began to collapse, the walls crumbling as the energy within them destabilized. Koda turned, his gaze meeting the alpha's for one final moment.

"This ends here," he said, his voice filled with quiet fury.

He turned and ran, the cavern collapsing behind him. The alpha's growls faded into the roar of falling stone as Koda emerged into the forest.

Chapter Nine:

THE MOON WAS HIGH, a swollen orb of silver light that painted the world in stark contrasts of shadow and glow. Koda stood at the edge of the cliff, the wind howling around him like a chorus of ancient voices. Below, the forest stretched out endlessly, its vast canopy a sea of black. Ahead, the alpha emerged from the shadows, its hulking form a silhouette against the moonlit sky.

The werewolf's golden eyes locked onto Koda, blazing with a mixture of hatred and primal hunger. It moved with a slow, deliberate gait, each step a declaration of its dominance. Behind it, the remaining pack gathered, their glowing eyes like embers dotting the darkness. But they stayed back. This was not their fight.

Koda's massive hands curled into fists. His breath was steady, his body aching but unyielding. He took a step forward, his presence radiating like the roots of the earth itself, unshakable and immovable.

The alpha stopped, its claws scraping against the stone as it lowered itself into a crouch. The wind seemed to still, the world holding its breath.

"You wanted this," Koda said, his voice low and steady, the rumble of a distant storm. *"Now, let's finish it."*

The alpha moved first, a blur of muscle and fury as it lunged. Koda met it head-on, their massive bodies colliding with the force of a thunderclap. The impact sent a shockwave through the ground, the stone beneath them cracking under their weight.

Koda swung his arm in a wide arc, his fist connecting with the alpha's ribs. The creature grunted but didn't falter, its claws flashing as they raked across Koda's chest. The gashes were deep, blood pouring down his fur in thick rivulets, but Koda didn't stagger.

Instead, he drove forward, slamming his shoulder into the alpha's chest and sending it sprawling across the ground. The werewolf rolled with the impact, its claws digging into the stone as it righted itself. It snarled, saliva dripping from its jagged teeth, and lunged again.

Koda sidestepped, his massive hand grabbing the alpha by the arm. With a roar, he swung the creature into a nearby boulder, the stone shattering under the force. The alpha yelped but twisted free, its claws slashing at Koda's side as it landed.

The two circled each other now, their breaths heavy, their bodies already battered. The pack watched from the shadows, their growls low and guttural.

"You're stronger than the others," Koda said, his voice calm despite the blood staining his fur. *"But strength alone won't save you."*

The alpha growled in response, its golden eyes narrowing as it prepared for the next strike.

The alpha charged again, its claws aiming for Koda's throat. Koda ducked, grabbing a massive rock from the ground and hurling it at the creature. The alpha dodged, but the rock smashed into the ground behind it, sending shards of stone flying in all directions.

Koda pressed his advantage, grabbing a nearby tree trunk that had fallen long ago. He swung it like a club, the wood creaking under the force. The alpha raised its arms to block, but the impact still sent it stumbling backward.

The ground beneath their feet shifted, the cliffside threatening to crumble under the weight of their battle. Koda felt the tremor and stepped back, his eyes scanning the terrain. The alpha took the opportunity to strike, its claws slashing at Koda's thigh. The pain was sharp and immediate, but Koda didn't falter.

He dropped the tree trunk and grabbed the alpha by the scruff of its neck, lifting it off the ground. The werewolf twisted and thrashed, its claws tearing at Koda's arms, but his grip was unyielding. With a roar, he slammed the creature into the ground, the stone cracking beneath it.

The alpha let out a guttural growl, its body coiling like a spring as it launched itself upward. Koda staggered as the creature tackled him, the two tumbling dangerously close to the edge of the cliff. The world seemed to tilt, the wind roaring as the ground gave way beneath them.

Koda grabbed at the rock face as they fell, his massive hand finding purchase on a jagged outcropping. The alpha clung to him, its claws digging into his shoulders as it snarled and snapped at his neck.

The wind whipped around them, the sound of the forest below a distant roar. Koda's muscles strained as he pulled himself upward, the alpha's weight making every movement a battle. The werewolf struck at him again, its claws tearing into his back.

With a roar of pain and fury, Koda swung his arm, smashing his fist into the alpha's face. The creature yelped, its grip loosening just enough for Koda to pull free. He grabbed the edge of the cliff and hauled himself up, his body heaving with exertion.

The alpha followed, its claws scraping against the rock as it climbed. Koda waited, his massive hands gripping a sharp boulder. As the werewolf's head crested the edge, he brought the rock down with all his might. The impact sent the alpha tumbling back, but it caught itself on the ledge below, its snarl echoing through the air.

"*You're stubborn,*" Koda growled, his breath heavy. "*But so am I.*"

The alpha leapt back onto the cliff, its movements slower now but no less feral. Blood dripped from its mouth and claws, its fur matted with dirt and gore. Koda stood tall, his massive frame battered but unbroken.

The two clashed again, their roars mingling with the howling wind. The alpha's claws found Koda's side, tearing into muscle, but Koda retaliated with a thunderous blow to its ribs. The werewolf staggered, and Koda pressed his advantage.

He grabbed the alpha by the arm, twisting until he heard the bone snap. The creature howled in pain, its claws flailing wildly. Koda didn't relent. He lifted the alpha off the ground and hurled it into a nearby tree, the trunk splitting under the force.

The pack growled from the shadows, their loyalty to the alpha holding them back but their fear of Koda growing. The forest seemed to tremble, the ground quaking under the weight of the battle.

The alpha rose unsteadily, its body trembling with exertion. Its golden eyes burned brighter, a final burst of fury and desperation driving it forward. It lunged at Koda with all its remaining strength, its claws and teeth aiming for his heart.

Koda met it head-on, his massive hands closing around its throat. The two struggled, their bodies locked in a deadly embrace. The alpha's claws tore into Koda's chest, but he didn't falter. He tightened his grip, his muscles straining as he lifted the creature off the ground.

With a roar that echoed across the forest, Koda slammed the alpha into the ground. The stone cracked and crumbled under the impact, the alpha's body going limp. Koda didn't stop. He grabbed the creature's jaws, his massive hands pulling them apart. The alpha let out one final, guttural growl before its head split in two.

The forest fell silent.

Koda stood over the alpha's lifeless body, his breath heavy, his wounds bleeding freely. The pack whimpered from the shadows, their glowing eyes filled with fear. One by one, they retreated into the forest, their bond to the alpha broken.

The wind calmed, the moonlight bathing the clearing in an eerie stillness. Koda knelt, his massive hand resting briefly on the alpha's chest. *"You were strong,"* he said quietly. *"But strength alone isn't enough."*

He rose slowly, his body aching but his resolve unshaken. The forest seemed to breathe again, its tension lifting as the balance was restored.

Chapter: Ten

The dawn broke softly over the forest, the golden light filtering through the trees and casting long shadows across the ground. The air was still, carrying the scent of pine and earth, and the forest seemed to exhale after holding its breath through the long night.

Koda moved slowly through the undergrowth, his massive form hunched slightly from the pain of his wounds. Blood matted his fur, and his muscles ached with every step, but he pressed on. Around him, the forest began to stir—birds calling tentatively, small animals emerging cautiously from their hiding places.

At the edge of a stream, Koda knelt, his massive hands cupping the cold water and splashing it over his face. The icy sting jolted him into focus, the rushing current carrying away the blood and dirt that clung to him.

"It's done," he murmured, his voice a low rumble that blended with the sound of the water. *"For now."*

Koda made his way back to the clearing where the battle had ended. The alpha's body lay still, its massive frame sprawled across the shattered ground. Koda paused, his gaze lingering on the lifeless form.

"You were a part of this forest once," he said quietly, his tone free of malice. *"But you forgot the balance. And that was your undoing."*

He knelt beside the body, his massive hands digging into the earth. With slow, deliberate movements, he began to bury the alpha, the soil rising to cover the creature that had once terrorized the forest. It wasn't a gesture of forgiveness—it was respect for what the alpha had been before its corruption.

As he finished, Koda stood, his eyes scanning the horizon. The pack was gone, scattered into the wilderness, their connection to the alpha broken. He knew they would not return—not for a long time.

The forest bore the scars of the battle. Trees lay shattered, their trunks splintered by the violence. The ground was churned and bloodied, the once-pristine clearing a reminder of what had been lost to restore balance.

Koda walked among the damage, his massive hands brushing against the broken trees. He could feel the forest's pain, its quiet mourning for what had been destroyed. But he could also feel its resilience, the quiet strength that would see it through.

"It always heals," he said softly. *"Given time."*

He paused at the edge of a small grove, where new shoots of grass were already pushing through the churned soil. It was a small sign, but it was enough.

By nightfall, Koda had found a place to rest. A small clearing, far from the site of the battle, where the forest hummed with life. He lit a fire—not out of need, but as a gesture of reflection. The flames danced, their light casting long shadows over the ground.

He sat with his back against a massive tree, his eyes fixed on the fire. His body ached, his wounds throbbed, but his mind was calm. The balance had been restored. For now.

"The forest always calls," he said quietly, as if speaking to someone unseen. *"And I always answer."*

His gaze shifted to the horizon, where the trees met the sky. The moon hung low, its light softer now, less imposing. Koda's voice dropped to a whisper, his words carrying into the stillness.

"But it's never over."

As the fire burned low, Koda leaned back, his eyes closing for the first time in what felt like days. The forest around him was quiet, its peace a fragile thing that he had fought to protect.

But the forest was never truly silent. In the distance, faint but unmistakable, came a sound. Not a howl. Not a growl. Something else. Something new.

Koda opened his eyes, his sharp gaze cutting through the darkness. He didn't move, but the faintest trace of a smile touched his lips.

"Not tonight," he murmured. *"But soon."*

Also by B. Humphrey

Bigfoot Vs
Bigfoot Vs Werewolves

Retro Horrors: The Lost Decade
Cassette Ghosts
Summer of the Black Star
The Arcade Incident
Dead End Drive – In
The Polaroid Project
Endless Paths: The Choose-Your-Own Doom Chronicles
Neon Dreams
The Forgotten Carnival
Satanic Panic
Skin of the Moon

The Autumn Folklore Chronicles
The Forest Of Forgotten Names
The Witch Of Windspindle Hollow

The Burrowfolk Chronicles

The Phantom Finders Club
A Haunting On Maplewood Street
The Secrets Of Old Fort Tower
Ghosts OF The Infirmary

The Starling Sleuths
Detective Starling vol. 1
Detective Starling Vol. 2

Winter Horrors
Whispers of the Wendigo
Cold Cuts
The Dark Beneath

Standalone
The Witch of Blackwood Hollow
The Storied Mind

Milton Keynes UK
Ingram Content Group UK Ltd.
UKHW020908291124
451807UK00013B/810